The Hidden One

By John J. Sutton

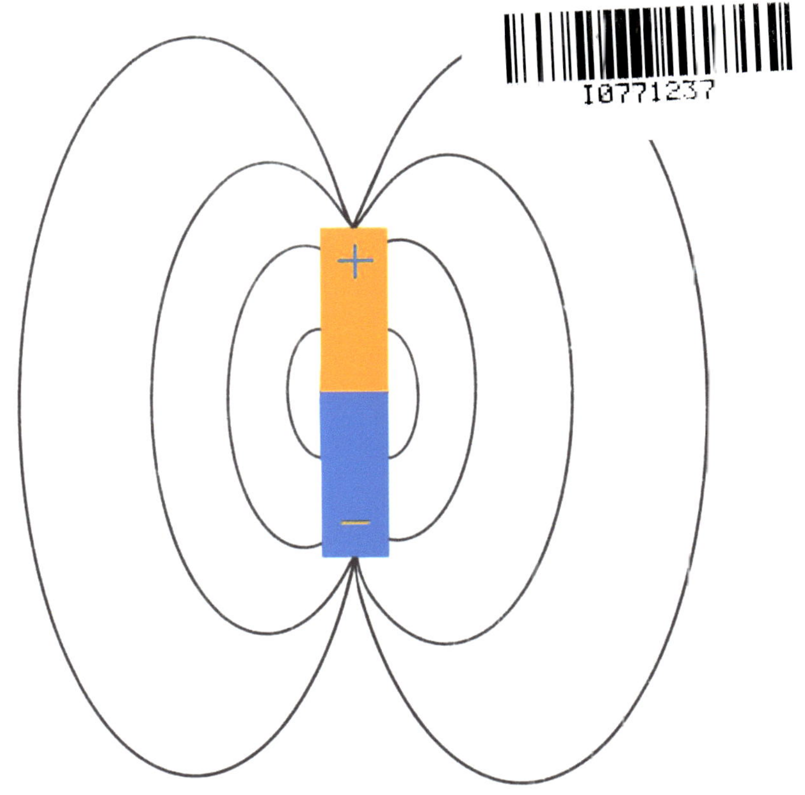

THE IRON TOOL THAT OPENED THE MOUTH OF THE GODS

Copyright © 2024

John J. Sutton

LCCN: 2024918419
eBook ISBN: 978-1-965683-79-8
Paper Back ISBN: 978-1-965683-80-4

All Rights Reserved. Any unauthorized reprint or use of this material is strictly prohibited. No part of this book may be reproduced or transmitted in any form or by any means, electronic or mechanical, including photocopying, recording, or by any information storage and retrieval system without express written permission from the author.

All reasonable attempts have been made to verify the accuracy of the information provided in this publication. Nevertheless, the author assumes no responsibility for any errors and/or omissions.

I have been going to write this book for almost 50 years. Although my research was complete in the mid-1970s, I have put off writing a book because I got a job and raised a family. Now that I am a grandparent, it's time for me to complete this task.

I am not one to embellish, so this book will be short and to the point.

If you are not interested in my dissection of western and eastern religions, you can jump to the "Tie That Binds" Chapter.

Most people, at one time or another, seek meaning in their lives, but usually it's when we become adults. In our early life, we are most likely exposed to some form of religious teaching. This was done to mold behavior and provide a moral framework. As a child, we don't know any different. We usually accept what we are taught and believe what we are told. Sometimes we may wonder or question what we are taught because certain things that we are told don't make sense. At that point, we have reached the age of reason. When we do question, sometimes we are met with resistance, which can lead to doubts as to what is true. When this happened to me, and I wasn't satisfied with the answer, it made me search for the answers.

As we are educated, we become aware of science and the laws of physics and mathematics. This is usually the first place we encounter conflicts with what we might have been told to believe and what is scientific fact. Some stick with what they were taught to believe, while others decide belief is not enough and go with science.

If all religion and science were suddenly destroyed today, science would come back the same way it is now because it is based on mathematics and the physical laws of the universe. However, religion would not come back the same way, because it is based on belief and not fact.

People often assert that religion's explanations of natural events originate from human attempts to make sense of the world. According to them, religion has to have a source and that source is usually a human attempting to explain some natural event. In science, the Big Bang theory is the explanation for the universe's beginning, but this theory too, raises the question of what caused the Big Bang.

The question is a valid one as it makes sense, because it's just not religion that has to have a source but the rule of thumb across every single discipline of science, across the entire world of rationality and logic is that a thing cannot cause itself. Like religion, science also looks for the source. We know that time cannot cause itself. Space cannot cause itself. Materials cannot cause themselves. Matter cannot cause itself. Energy cannot cause itself. You need something extremely powerful outside of energy, outside of time (therefore timeless), outside of matter (therefore immaterial) to cause it.

Prior to my research, I wondered if science and religion were fundamentally at odds with each other, each existing in its own realm without any overlap. Science, with its rigorous methods and empirical evidence, seemed to be a world apart from the faith and spiritual teachings of religion. However, my perspective began to change when I started to study these two disparate fields more deeply.

Anyone who wants to study different religions accurately should start by blocking all the noise and rumors they've heard about them. Read the Scriptures yourself instead of learning the religion from people who seemingly appear to practice them. If you want to genuinely understand a religion, first read their Holy Book. Do not watch the news or seek information from Instagram or YouTube reels from Influencers, rather, just clear your mind, open that Holy Book, and read the words yourself, because when I started to do exactly this, I saw some alignment between the two. The more I researched, the more I discovered a basic scientific principle that actually supports and echo the wisdom found in some of the scriptures. Science and Religion seem to be in stark contrast with each other, but this is not always the case.

Science and religion are not always mutually exclusive but can complement and reinforce each other. In the chapters ahead, I will further share the research and insights that led to this conclusion. I will also shed light on how the pursuit of scientific knowledge can coexist with and even enhance religious faith, providing a more holistic understanding of the world and our place in it.

There are so many religions. Depending on where you grew up, you may encounter different ones. They all have some unique beliefs, and they all use rules to regulate people's behavior. Sometimes there is a figurehead or leader.

Despite the differences, we find many religions borrowed from one another or share concepts. Many times the newer religions try to hide where they got their concepts. For me, I was most interested in what was the same in the various religions instead of what was different.

The Big Three

For the western world, there are three great religions that dominate the belief space. These are Judaism, Christianity, and Islam. In 2022, Statista published a report that showed the percentages of people following different religions around the world. Around 31.6% of the global population were identified as Christian. Around 25.8% of the global population identified as Muslims, 15.1% of the global populations as Hindu, and 0.2% as Jews. These religions originated in the same area of the world, the Middle East, and they are related.

Judaism is the oldest of the three and contains a history and wisdom of a people who were once nomads. Later, they found a home of their own through the worship of Yahwey and the leadership of Moses who lead the Jewish people out of the bondage of Egypt. The history and wisdom of the Jewish people is contained in the old testament of the bible.

Christianity was second, which originated from the Jewish people and was predicted in the old testament of the bible. Jesus the Christ was predicted to be a Jewish Messiah. The new testament of the bible is the story of his life.

A little more than 600 years after Christ, the Islamic prophet Muhammad created the Islamic religion. Islam expressed itself as a return to the original faith as passed down from Abraham, Moses, and Jesus. Muslims call for the submission to the one true God, Allah, and to prepare for the last day of judgment.

Contents

THE BIBLE

The Bible is a book composed of two parts, the Old Testament before Christ, and the New Testament after Christ. The Old Testament is thought to be an approximate history of the Jewish people, but contains symbolic language describing things such as the creation of the world. There are a lot of questions that come up concerning the creation story. Some take the story as a literal truth, while others do not. There is much war and violence in the Old Testament with killing in the name of god. There is also much beauty in the Psalms, especially Chapter 3 of Ecclesiastes, Verses 1 through 8.

Here, the balance of life is expressed through the contrast of opposites. In Isaiah 45:7, it says, "I form the light and created darkness, I make peace and create evil: I the lord do all these things." I am Alpha and Omega, the first and the last. This verse shows that God is the creator of everything, both good and bad. It expresses the balance of life—the light and the darkness, peace and hardship. It's a powerful reminder that everything, even struggles and challenges, comes under God's control. All of these express the contrast of opposites. In most of the Scriptures, God and the Devil were considered to be opposite forces, where one was good, and the other evil.

The New Testament is the story of Jesus the Christ who was predicted to be a Jewish Messiah, but it didn't work out that way. Jesus turned away from war and violence, and instead embraced peace, love and treating your neighbor as yourself. This was a departure from the Old Testament where God could be at times a vengeful God. Instead, God was supposed to be a loving caring God. Jesus said, "Love the Lord your God with all your heart and with all your soul and with all your mind. This is the first and greatest commandment. And the second is like it, Love your neighbor as yourself." From Matthew 5-7, I believe Jesus expressed it best at the Sermon on the Mount. Jesus referenced the duality concept in many references. Matthew 7:1,2 – 16:25 – 18:4 – 19:30 – 20:16 – 20:27 – 23:11,12. For whatever a man soweth, that he shall also reap. Also, Luke 6:37 says, "Judge not and you shall not be judged. Condemn not, and you shall not be condemned. Forgive, and you shall be forgiven." Jesus teaches here that we shouldn't judge others, because the way we treat others will be how we are treated. If we are harsh and unforgiving, we'll receive the same in return. It's a call for kindness, understanding, and mercy.

One of the more interesting Jesus quotes is in St. Mark 9:37-39. John answered him, saying: Master we saw one casting out devils in thy name, one who followeth not us, and we forbad him. But Jesus said: Do not forbid him, for there is no man that doth a miracle in my name that can soon speak ill of me. For he that is not against you is for you. Jesus is saying that people who are doing good, even if they don't belong to your group, are still on the same side. As long as they are not opposing you, they are contributing to good.

From what I have learned, all the great prophets—whether from Judaism, Christianity, Islam, or other faiths— were mostly men of peace, love and understanding. Forgiveness was a release from hatred. Most all of them acknowledged the natural law of balance and sought to maintain it.

They sought to guide humanity toward a higher moral and spiritual path, emphasizing compassion and empathy. Forgiveness, in their teachings, was seen as a powerful release from hatred and bitterness, a way to heal relationships and build harmony. In Islam, for example, Prophet Muhammad preached peace, advocating for mercy and reconciliation. In Christianity, Jesus Christ emphasized love, famously teaching to "turn the other cheek" and to love one's enemies, demonstrating that peace is stronger than vengeance. Moses, despite leading the Israelites through difficult trials, advocated for justice, patience, and humility before God.

A common theme among these prophets was the recognition of balance and duality in life—between good and evil, light and darkness, and action and reflection. They acknowledged the natural law of balance, encouraging their followers to seek equilibrium in their actions. This idea can be found in teachings like the golden rule ("Do unto others as you would have them do unto you") and the concept of karma in Hinduism and Buddhism, which reflects the idea that actions have consequences that ripple through time.

Moreover, many prophets also called for social justice, promoting the protection of the vulnerable, such as widows, orphans, and the poor, recognizing that peace could only be achieved when society as a whole embraced fairness and compassion. Whether in the Torah, the Bible, the Quran, or other sacred texts, these leaders modeled a way of living that transcended personal ego and embraced a higher, more connected form of existence.

Ultimately, through their lives and teachings, many prophets not only brought messages from the divine but also embodied the ideals of peace, love, forgiveness, and balance, showing humanity how to navigate the complexities of life with grace and purpose.

However, in the ancient scriptures there are cases in each religion where violence is used against enemies and is justified in the name of God.

THE QURAN

The Quran is a mix of beautiful thoughts about God and people, but also contains harsh consequences if one is not faithful to the way of Islam. The core of Islam teaches that the previous Jewish and Christian faiths must be brought back to the true religion preached by Abraham, that is, the absolute submission to the will of God, Allah.

Allah is almighty and all-knowing, and although compassionate towards his creation, he is stern in retribution. The Quran itself preaches the oneness of God and emphasizes divine mercy and forgiveness. Muhammad the prophet, believed he was a messenger from God, who was to confirm previous scriptures. He taught that God revealed his will to the Jewish and Christian people, but they disobeyed God's commandments. The Jewish people were accused of corrupting the scriptures, and the Christians of committing blasphemy by worshiping Jesus as the Son of God. One of the teachings of the Quran was that no human could be the son of God.

Jewish and Christians alike were described as "people of the book". As such they were considered unbelievers if they did not submit and recognize Islam as the one true religion. According to the Quran, unbelievers were not to be harmed, but if one was living in a country ruled by Islam, they could be taxed. In more recent times, extremists have said unbelievers can be killed. "I am the relenting one, the merciful. But the infidels who die unbelievers shall incur the curse of God, the angels, and all mankind. Under it they shall remain forever; their punishment shall not be mitigated, nor shall they be reprieved." (The Cow 2: 162)

The Quran had it's own set of rules similar to the 10 commandments, but more refined. "Fight for the sake of God those that fight against you, but do not attack them first. God does not love aggressors." (The

Cow 2:191- 2:192) "Those that have faith and do good works, attend to their prayers and render the alms levy, will be rewarded by their Lord and will have nothing to fear or regret." (The Cow: 2: 277)

"To God belongs all that the heavens and the earth contain. Whether you reveal your thoughts or hide them, God will bring you to account for them. He will forgive whom he will and punish whom he pleases; God has power over all things." (The Cow 2: 285)

THE TORAH

The Torah, also known as the Pentateuch, is the central and most sacred text of Judaism. It is a cornerstone of Jewish religious life and thought, and its teachings have profoundly influenced not only Judaism but also Christianity and Islam. The Torah consists of the first five books of the Hebrew Bible: Genesis, Exodus, Leviticus, Numbers, and Deuteronomy. These books contain a mixture of narrative history, laws, ethical teachings, and religious rituals that have guided Jewish life for millennia.

The Torah is traditionally believed to have been revealed to Moses, one of the most important prophets in Judaism, around the 13th century BCE. According to Jewish tradition, Moses received the Torah directly from God on Mount Sinai, shortly after leading the Israelites out of slavery in Egypt. This event, known as the Sinai Revelation, is considered the most significant moment in Jewish history because it established the covenant between God and the people of Israel.

Moses is a central figure in Judaism, Christianity, and Islam. In the Torah, Moses is depicted as a leader, lawgiver, and prophet who played a crucial role in the foundation of the Jewish faith. He is credited with transmitting God's commandments to the Israelites. He guided them through their 40-year journey in the wilderness, and lead them to the edge of the Promised Land.

The Torah emphasizes the idea of monotheism—the belief in one, all-powerful, and compassionate God who created the universe and continues to be actively involved in its governance. This belief sets Judaism apart from the polytheistic religions that were prevalent in the ancient Near East.

One of the key themes in the Torah is the concept of covenant, or "brit" in Hebrew. This covenant is a sacred agreement between God and the

Israelites, in which God promises to be their protector and guide, and in return, the Israelites commit to following God's commandments. The Torah outlines these commandments, which include both moral and ritual laws, covering aspects of daily life, ethical behavior, and religious practice.

The Emphasis on Law and Ethical Conduct

The Torah places significant emphasis on law and ethical conduct, reflecting the belief that living a life in accordance with God's commandments is the path to holiness. The laws of the Torah, known as mitzvot, cover a wide range of areas, including justice, charity, honesty, family relations, and community responsibilities. These laws are not merely legal codes but are seen as divine instructions for living a righteous life.

One of the most famous ethical teachings in the Torah is found in Leviticus 19:18, which states, "You shall love your neighbor as yourself." This commandment underscores the importance of treating others with kindness, compassion, and respect. The Torah's emphasis on social justice and ethical behavior has had a lasting impact on Jewish thought and has influenced the development of Western legal and moral systems.

Key Verses from the Torah

Several verses from the Torah encapsulate its core messages and themes.

For example:

- **Genesis 1:1**: "In the beginning, God created the heavens and the earth." This verse introduces the idea of a single Creator who is the source of all life and existence.

- **Exodus 20:2-3**: "I am the Lord your God, who brought you out of the land of Egypt, out of the house of bondage. You shall have no other gods before Me." These verses introduce the Ten Commandments, which are central to the Torah's ethical teachings.

- **Deuteronomy 6:4-5**: "Hear, O Israel: The Lord our God, the Lord is one. You shall love the Lord your God with all your heart, with all your soul, and with all your might." This passage, known as the Shema, is a declaration of the oneness of God and the devotion that the Israelites are to have toward Him.

The Origins of Judaism

The Torah serves as a religious text and as a historical account of the origins of Judaism. It traces the lineage of the Jewish people from the patriarchs—Abraham, Isaac, and Jacob—through their enslavement in Egypt, and their eventual liberation and journey to the Promised Land under the leadership of Moses. The narratives of the Torah establish the foundational events and figures of Judaism, providing a sense of identity and purpose for the Jewish people.

Judaism, as it originated from the teachings of the Torah, is one of the oldest monotheistic religions in the world. The Torah's influence extends beyond religious practices, shaping Jewish culture, traditions, and values. It has also played a significant role in the development of later religious traditions, including Christianity and Islam, both of which revere the Torah as a sacred text.

SIMILARITIES BETWEEN RELIGIONS

Islam, Judaism, and Christianity are three major religions that have a lot in common. They all believe in one God and trace their roots back to the same ancestor, Abraham. These religions share many similar beliefs, values, and traditions. This chapter will look at the similarities between Islam, Judaism, and Christianity, showing how they are connected. By understanding these common points, we can see how these religions are united and can respect each other more.

I found verses in both the Bible and the Quran that encourage wisdom, understanding, and the pursuit of knowledge—principles that are also at the heart of scientific inquiry.

For example, in **Proverbs 4:7**, it is said, "The beginning of wisdom is this: Get wisdom. Though it cost all you have, get understanding." Here, the verse emphasizes the importance of seeking wisdom and understanding, which can be interpreted as valuing knowledge and reasoning.

In the Quran, in **Surah Yaseen (36:62),** God says, "And he had already led astray from among you much of creation, so did you not use reason?"

To draw similarities between the religions, let's start by the Word **"God"** itself.

We know that Jesus spoke Aramaic. In Aramaic, the word for God is "Elah". In Arabic, the language in which the Quran was revealed to Prophet Muhammad, the word for God is "Allah" (الله), which means the Only One True God. In Hebrew, the word for God is "Eloah" (אֱלֹהַּ).

These religions have more in common than just the literal Word of God.

Below is a comparison table of the similarities below for an in-depth analysis:

ASPECT	ISLAM	JUDAISM	CHRISTIANITY
Monotheism	Believes in the oneness of God (Allah), who is all-powerful and all-knowing.	Emphasizes the belief in a single, indivisible God (YHWH).	Teaches the belief in one God, though in the context of the Trinity (Father, Son, Holy Spirit).
Prophets and Revelation	Believes in a line of prophets including Adam, Noah, Abraham, Moses, and Jesus, culminating in Muhammad, who received the final revelation, the Quran.	Recognizes many prophets, including Abraham and Moses, who conveyed God's will and laws.	Accepts the prophets of the Old Testament and believes that Jesus Christ is the ultimate revelation of God.

ASPECT	ISLAM	JUDAISM	CHRISTIANITY
Holy Scriptures	The Quran is considered the final and complete revelation from God.	The Tanakh (including the Torah, Prophets, and Writings) is the central reference of religious Judaic tradition.	The Bible, which includes the Old Testament (shared with Judaism) and the New Testament, documents the life and teachings of Jesus Christ.
Ethical Teachings	Emphasizes justice, compassion, charity (Zakat), and moral conduct.	Focuses on ethical living, justice, charity (Tzedakah), and adherence to the commandments.	Teaches love, forgiveness, charity, and moral integrity, with a strong emphasis on loving one's neighbor.
Concept of Afterlife	Believes in life after death, including Heaven (Jannah) and Hell (Jahannam), based on one's deeds.	Beliefs about the afterlife vary; some texts speak of a world to come or resurrection.	Believes in eternal life, with Heaven and Hell as outcomes based on one's relationship with God.

ASPECT	ISLAM	JUDAISM	CHRISTIANITY
Prayer and Worship	Daily prayers (Salah) are a central practice, along with other acts of worship.	Daily prayers and observance of the Sabbath and other religious rituals are integral.	Prayer, worship services, and sacraments like Baptism and Communion are essential practices.

Islam, Judaism, and Christianity are very similar, especially in their core beliefs about God and how we should live our lives. They all worship one powerful and merciful God and promote values like compassion, justice, and truth, and it's sad to see conflicts and divisions arise because of religious differences when these faiths share so much common ground.

These conflicts often hide the shared values that could bring people together. I firmly believe that by focusing on what we have in common, we can create a more peaceful and inclusive world where religious beliefs unite us instead of dividing us.

However, the Western religions, Christianity, Judaism, and Islam, each claim to be the only truth or the only path sanctioned by God. I have found verses from the Bible, Torah (as part of the Jewish tradition), and Quran that convey the idea of these faiths being the true path.

Christianity (The Bible):

- **John 14:6 (NIV):**

- *Jesus answered, "I am the way and the truth and the life. No one comes to the Father except through me."*

- **Acts 4:12 (NIV)**:

- *"Salvation is found in no one else, for there is no other name under heaven given to mankind by which we must be saved."*

Judaism (The Torah/Tanakh):

- **Deuteronomy 6:4 (Shema Yisrael)**:

- *"Hear, O Israel: The Lord our God, the Lord is one."*

- **Exodus 20:3 (NIV)**:

- *"You shall have no other gods before me."*

Islam (The Quran):

Imrans 3:19: *"The only true faith in God's eyes is Islam."*

Imrans 3:85: *"And whoever desires other than Islam as religion - never will it be accepted from him, and he, in the Hereafter, will be among the losers."*

The Eastern religions, however, avoid such claims.

EXPLORING OTHER OPTIONS

With the big three, I was left wanting. There was too much violence and intolerance in them. Pretty much their attitude was if you didn't think or believe what they did, you were wrong and were going to suffer for it, sometimes at their own hands. That didn't inspire me.

Although there were a lot of good things I read, the underlying theme of all three was there was a simple choice. Heaven or Hell. Obey the rules and you go to heaven, disobey and you go to hell. So what about the forgiving God?

God forgives whom he pleases, and punishes those who he chooses.

There was some commonality. You reap what you sow. The law of Karma and the law of physics, for every action there is an opposite reaction. God is some unseen power we must worship and accept whatever occurs to us. It is the will of God. Bad things happen to good people, and good things happen to bad people.

Most of us accept the idea that we suffer the consequences of our actions. This is evident in our lives all the time. Sometimes it is not readily apparent, but sooner or later, we will experience the consequences. There is also random interaction. You can be minding your own business and then you die suddenly in a car wreck. Then there are children dying of starvation in war zones or in drought-stricken areas of the world. God does what he pleases!

I can understand why atheists don't believe in a god.

So I asked myself, what else is there? Because of the people I met in my life, I discovered that there was more to the story and there are different ways of thinking. I found that in eastern religions. Growing up, I was pretty much unaware of them, but as I matured and started asking questions that went unanswered I wanted to learn about them. So I continued my search for answers there.

Hinduism

The Hindu sacred symbol above represents the "Om" mantra in meditation and is a focal point in Hinduism. It is said to be the essence of the supreme absolute consciousness. It is a sound of God or the divine. It is found many times in the Upanishads and other Hindu texts and is also a tool for meditation. It is said that the syllable may hold the mind in focus on the concepts of the first cause, the essence of self-knowledge.

Hinduism is one of the world's oldest religions. It is complex and describes many aspects of nature in the form of many gods. The supreme god was Brahman. Everything is part of and created by Brahman, the ultimate reality. Brahman's expression and power were represented by a large diversity of gods/deities, which come from the

Brahman. Similar to Christianity, there was a trinity. Brahman the creator, Vishnu the preserver, and Shiva the destroyer.

This trinity is a representation of the duality of nature, but also shows a relationship and the contrast between two opposing forces. This is an important concept, which comes up in other religious systems as well.

Hinduism also has a Christ-like figure named Krishna, who was worshiped as the Hindu god Vishnu and as the supreme god. In the "song of God," the Bhagavad Gita, his incarnation and contemplation of his attributes are considered preparation for the knowledge of the Godhead. This is very similar to Jesus Christ in his relationship to the "father" which in Hindu terms would be Brahman.

In the Hindu term for avatar, a god becomes a man. Applying the concept of an avatar, Jesus would be a deity belonging to the fourth layer of gods beneath the main three Hindu gods. Krishna was on the same fourth level and was an avatar. One major difference between Jesus and Krishna was their attitude toward war. The Bhagavad Gita is a Hindu scripture where Krishna discusses the ethics of war with the Pandava warrior prince, Arjuna. Krishna tells Arjuna he must understand his dharma or duty. Krishna wants Arjuna to realize that by being a warrior, he can find a greater purpose in engaging in a righteous war regardless of the outcome. This is in conflict with the teachings of Jesus Christ who instead preached to turn the other cheek and forgo retaliation for personal offenses. Most pragmatic people would agree that Jesus Christ is the ideal, but Krishna is the harsh reality.

What is most important to me in Hinduism is the expression of the idea of a creative force, Brahman, which expresses itself through opposing forces Vishnu (positive) and Shiva (negative). Hinduism also gives us the guidelines for mediation where one can reach an understanding of the universe by focusing on Om. A slimmed-down version of this is transcendental meditation, which also originated in India.

I found Hinduism to be rich in symbolism but a bit complex with all the various gods and deities. One can get caught up in the complex systems of religions, but I prefer the basic simple concepts that don't distract

Buddhism

Buddha means the awakened one, or the enlightened one. Here is a guy from a wealthy family who was sheltered from the world, but who went out on his own to see what was beyond his palace. He saw people suffering and wondered why. He denounced his rich life to live as a wandering monk. He fasted and endured hardship until he realized the "middle way" between pleasure and pain, which lead him to Nirvana, which is the freedom from ignorance, craving, and suffering. The teaching of the Buddha was a way of liberation with the sole purpose of experiencing Nirvana. The Buddha did not subscribe to a system that tried to explain the universe and it's cause. When he was pressed for answers regarding the origin of the world and the self, he gave no answer. He said the questions were irrelevant, and did not lead to liberation or Nirvana.

The path is the middle way, or the balance. Buddha realized that unity is achieved through meditating and finding the middle way. Perfect balance is the way to Nirvana.

The Buddha became the model of what could be achieved by right thinking.

Zen is forgetting oneself in the act of uniting with the universal being. Similar to Hinduism this is achieved through meditation and mental exercises to free the mind. There is much practice and concentration on meditation. You must sit with a mind that is relaxed and open.

The way of Zen is striving for the Bodhisattva ideal, which is one who wishes to gain Enlightenment for the sake of all beings. For anyone wishing to follow the path, one must develop inner calm and have a positive outlook that leads to true wisdom. This is a balance created by an active concern for others, which leads to great compassion. The Avatars of the great religions are examples of this ideal.

For a Zen Buddhist, the ordinary person is the Buddha. The ordinary mind is the middle way. Zen people carry on ordinary lives and do not call attention to themselves. They do not put on wise or superior air. They realize all things are empty but carry the seeds of growth. "Let your light shine before men that they may see your good works." As in the Bible, you will know them by their fruits.

I highly recommend reading "The Way of Zen" by Alan Watts. This excellent book goes into much more detail and ties the many eastern philosophies together

Taoism

Taoism is a tradition, which originated in China. It is considered both a philosophy and a religion. It is connected to the philosopher Lao Tzu, who lived around 500 BC, and who wrote the main book on Taoism. Taoism believes that humans and nature live in balance with the universe. Tao is the path or the way. Taoists believe in immortality where the human spirit or soul joins the harmony of the universe after death.

The symbol above represents the universe spinning in motion where the positive and the negative flow together in balance. Each side contains the seed of the other. This is the basic building block of the universe, the unity of opposites. From it all else follows.

There are four basic principles of Taoism. The first was simplicity, patience and compassion. Number two was going with the flow. "When nothing is done, nothing is left undone." Third was letting go. "If you

realize all things change, there is nothing you will try and hold on to."
Fourth is Harmony.

Like Buddhism and Zen, Taoism is about balance or the middle way. The Tao symbol represents this balance. Likewise Hinduism expresses the same concept with Brahman (the whole symbol), Vishnu and Shiva (the two opposing forces). Here we see the basic building block of the universe, expressed in a symbol.

A COMPARISON OF ASIAN RELIGIONS

Hinduism, Buddhism, Zen, and Taoism are four prominent philosophies and religions that originated in Asia, each offering unique perspectives on the path to enlightenment, the nature of reality, and the way we should live our lives.

Despite their differences, these traditions share common themes, such as the importance of meditation, the pursuit of spiritual liberation, and a focus on living in harmony with the natural world. The following table compares key aspects of these four traditions, highlighting both their shared principles and their distinct approaches to spirituality.

ASPECT	HINDUISM	BUDDHISM	ZEN	TAOISM
Origin	India, around 1500 BCE	India, around 6th century BCE	Japan, 6th century CE	China, around 4th century BCE
Key Texts	Vedas, Upanishads, Bhagavad Gita	Tripitaka, Mahayana Sutras	No central texts; teachings of Zen masters	Tao Te Ching, Zhuangzi

Core Belief	Dharma (duty), karma, samsara (rebirth), moksha (liberation)	Four Noble Truths, Eightfold Path, Nirvana	Meditation (Zazen), direct insight	The Tao (the Way), Wu Wei (non-action)
Concept of God	Polytheistic (many gods), Brahman (ultimate reality)	Generally non-theistic, focuses on individual enlightenment	Non-theistic, focuses on direct experience of reality	Non-theistic, focuses on harmony with the Tao
Goal of Life	Achieving moksha (liberation from the cycle of rebirth)	Attaining Nirvana (liberation from suffering)	Satori (sudden enlightenment)	Achieving harmony with the Tao and the natural world
View on Afterlife	Reincarnation until moksha is achieved	Reincarnation until Nirvana is attained	Focus on the present moment rather than afterlife	Afterlife not emphasized; focus on life in harmony

Moral Code	Dharma (righteous living), Ahimsa (non-violence)	Eightfold Path (right conduct, right livelihood, etc.)	Living in the present moment, mindfulness	Living according to the Tao, naturalness, simplicity
Rituals and Practices	Yoga, meditation, puja (worship)	Meditation, mindfulness, monastic living	Zazen (sitting meditation), Koans (riddles)	Meditation, Tai Chi, feng shui, alchemy
View on Suffering	Suffering is due to karma and attachment	Suffering (Dukkha) is inherent in life; can be overcome	Suffering is due to delusion and attachment	Suffering is due to not living in harmony with the Tao
Spiritual Teachers	Gurus, Sages	Buddha, Lamas, Monks	Zen Masters, Roshi	Laozi, Zhuangzi, Immortals

When we compare Hinduism, Buddhism, Zen, and Taoism, we find that each offers unique ideas about life, the path to enlightenment, and how we should live. Hinduism talks about the cycle of life and reaching liberation through karma, duty, and devotion. Buddhism teaches us to overcome suffering and find peace through the Four Noble Truths and the Eightfold Path. Zen, a form of Buddhism, focuses on simple, direct experiences and meditation, while Taoism encourages living in harmony with the natural flow of the universe, known as the Tao.

Even though these religions are different, they all emphasize being mindful, understanding that life is ever-changing, and finding inner peace. The main takeaway is that while there are different paths to spiritual fulfillment, the goal is often the same: finding balance, wisdom, and peace within ourselves. These teachings remind us that true understanding can come from looking at the world from different perspectives and bringing them together.

DIFFERENCES BETWEEN RELIGIONS: EAST AND WEST

While Islam, Judaism, Christianity, and Hinduism share some common themes and principles, they also differ in significant ways. For instance, Islam, Judaism, and Christianity are rooted in monotheism, with a belief in one God, though they differ in their interpretations of God's nature and the role of prophets. In contrast, Hinduism presents a more complex view, with beliefs ranging from polytheism to a more abstract monotheism, depending on the tradition within Hinduism.

The holy texts of these religions—such as the Quran, Torah, Bible, and Hindu scriptures—also differ in content, structure, and purpose. These differences influence how followers view the afterlife, salvation, and the moral and ethical codes they follow in daily life. Additionally, each religion has its own set of rituals, practices, and clerical structures that guide the spiritual lives of its adherents.

The below comparison table highlights the key differences between these religions.

ASPECT	ISLAM	JUDAISM	CHRISTIANITY	HINDUISM
Concept of God	Monotheism: Belief in one God (Allah).	Monotheism: Belief in one God (Yahweh).	Monotheism: Belief in one God, with the Trinity concept (Father, Son, Holy Spirit).	Polytheism/Monotheism: Belief in many gods (Brahma, Vishnu, Shiva) or one supreme reality (Brahman).
Prophets	Belief in prophets, including Muhammad as the final prophet.	Belief in prophets, such as Moses.	Belief in prophets, with Jesus as the Son of God and the savior.	Sages such as Krishna are highly revered.
Holy Book	Quran.	Torah (part of the Hebrew Bible).	Bible (Old Testament and New Testament).	Multiple texts, including the Vedas, Upanishads, Bhagavad Gita, and others.
Salvation	Achieved through faith in Allah, good deeds, and following the Five Pillars.	Achieved through obedience to God's laws and commandments.	Achieved through faith in Jesus Christ as the savior.	Achieved through karma, dharma, and the cycle of reincarnation (samsara).
Afterlife	Belief in Heaven (Jannah) and Hell (Jahannam); afterlife is eternal.	Belief in the afterlife, with a focus on the World to Come (Olam Ha-Ba).	Belief in Heaven and Hell; eternal life through Jesus.	Reincarnation and moksha (liberation from the cycle of rebirth).

ASPECT	ISLAM	JUDAISM	CHRISTIANITY	HINDUISM
Rituals and Practices	Five Pillars of Islam (Shahada, Salat, Zakat, Sawm, Hajj).	Observance of the Sabbath, kosher laws, and other commandments.	Sacraments, prayer, and worship, with varying practices among denominations.	Diverse rituals depending on the tradition, including puja (worship), meditation, and yoga.
Views on Jesus	Jesus is a prophet, not divine.	Jesus is not a prophet or the Messiah.	Jesus is the Son of God, the Messiah, and the savior.	Jesus is seen as an enlightened teacher, but not as central to Hindu beliefs.
Original Sin	No concept of original sin; humans are born innocent.	No concept of original sin; humans are born with free will.	Belief in original sin, redeemed by Jesus' sacrifice.	No concept of original sin; emphasis on karma from past lives.
Clergy	Imams and scholars (Ulama).	Rabbis and priests (Kohanim).	Priests, pastors, ministers, and bishops.	Priests (Brahmins) and spiritual leaders (gurus).
Views on Other Religions	Generally recognizes previous Abrahamic religions but sees Islam as the final and complete revelation.	Sees Judaism as the true faith for Jews, with no need to convert others.	Missionary activity aimed at spreading Christianity; views other religions as incomplete without Christ.	Accepts multiple paths to the divine; generally non-proselytizing.

The table allows us to quickly identify what sets each religion apart, making it clear how their teachings and traditions have evolved in different cultural and historical contexts. This structured format helps simplify complex ideas and provides a clear overview of some unique aspects of each faith.

UNITY OF OPPOSITES

"The first shall be last, and the last shall be first."

The Universal Law of Balance and Consequences

Humans have sought to understand the world around them, leading to the development of different philosophies, religions, and scientific principles. Surprisingly, despite their varied origins, many of these ideas share a common thread—a belief in balance and consequences. Whether it's through the concept of Yin and Yang, the principle of "you reap what you sow," Newton's third law of motion, or the Hindu law of Karma, the idea that every action has a corresponding reaction is a universal truth that resonates across cultures and disciplines.

Yin and Yang: The Balance of Opposites

The ancient Chinese philosophy of Yin and Yang is one of the earliest representations of balance. Yin and Yang are two opposite but unified forces that make up everything in the universe. Yin represents darkness, femininity, and passivity, while Yang symbolizes light, masculinity, and activity. According to this philosophy, everything in life is a balance between these two unified forces. When Yin and Yang are in harmony, life is in balance; when they are out of balance, it leads to chaos and disorder.

In simple terms, Yin and Yang teach us that there is always a need for balance in life. For example, too much work without rest (Yang without Yin) can lead to burnout, while too much rest without work (Yin without Yang) can lead to stagnation. This concept isn't just about opposites; it's about understanding that life's challenges and successes are interconnected, and both are necessary for a balanced life. The unity between Yin and Yang is expressed in the universe.

Yin and Yang, and the Bible

"For everything there is a season, and a time for every matter under heaven: a time to be born, and a time to die; a time to plant, and a time to pluck up what is planted; a time to kill, and a time to heal; a time to break down, and a time to build up; a time to weep, and a time to laugh; a time to mourn, and a time to dance; a time to throw away stones, and a time to gather stones together; a time to embrace, and a time to refrain from embracing; a time to seek, and a time to lose; a time to keep, and a time to throw away; a time to tear, and a time to sew; a time to keep silence, and a time to speak; a time to love, and a time to hate; a time for war, and a time for peace." (Ecclesiastes 3, 1-8)

The verse from Ecclesiastes (3:1-8) beautifully captures the ebb and flow of life, highlighting how every moment has its opposite. For every action or emotion, there is a counterbalance—a natural rhythm to existence. This concept closely aligns with the idea of yin and yang from Eastern philosophy.

In yin and yang, two seemingly opposite forces are interconnected and interdependent. Yin represents qualities like darkness, passivity, and rest, while yang embodies light, activity, and energy. Just as the verse in Ecclesiastes contrasts birth with death, planting with uprooting, and love with hate, yin and yang illustrate how these opposites are not only necessary but also complementary.

For example, in the verse, "a time to weep, and a time to laugh," we see that joy and sorrow are both parts of life. Similarly, in yin and yang, one cannot exist without the other—joy (yang) gains its meaning in contrast to sorrow (yin), and vice versa. This duality is essential for balance in life.

The verse "a time to love, and a time to hate; a time for war, and a time for peace" echoes the yin and yang concept even more strongly. Love and hate, war and peace, though opposites, are part of the same cycle. They don't just exist separately; they define and influence each other.

Both the positive and negative experiences are necessary to create balance and understanding in our lives.

"You Reap What You Sow": A Moral Principle

In Christianity and other Abrahamic religions, the idea that "you reap what you sow" is a guiding moral principle. This phrase, found in the Bible, essentially means that the actions you take will eventually come back to you, whether for good or bad. If you plant seeds of kindness, generosity, and honesty, you will harvest positive outcomes. Conversely, if you plant seeds of deceit, cruelty, or greed, you will eventually face the consequences of those actions.

This principle serves as a reminder that our choices have consequences, and those consequences are directly related to the nature of our actions. It encourages people to live with integrity, knowing that what they do today will shape their future.

Newton's Third Law: Action and Reaction

Similarly, in the world of science, Sir Isaac Newton's third law of motion states, "For every action, there is an equal and opposite reaction." This law, while originally applied to the physical world, can also be understood in a broader context. It echoes the idea that every action we take has a corresponding effect, much like the moral and philosophical teachings examples.

For instance, if you push against a wall, the wall pushes back with equal force. This law is a clear representation of balance in the physical world. But beyond physics, it reminds us that our actions—whether they be physical, emotional, or moral—will always produce an outcome. It's a scientific validation of the cause-and-effect principle that's found in spiritual teachings.

Karma: The Hindu Concept of Moral Balance

The Hindu concept of Karma is perhaps the most well-known representation of cause and effect in spiritual terms. Karma teaches that every action, thought, or word carries energy, and this energy eventually returns to the individual in some form. Good actions lead to good Karma, bringing positive outcomes, while bad actions lead to bad Karma, resulting in suffering or challenges.

Karma is often misunderstood as immediate retribution or reward, but in reality, it's about the long-term balance of our deeds. It suggests that our current life circumstances are the result of our past actions, and what we do now will shape our future. Karma encourages mindfulness, as it makes us aware that every choice we make contributes to our destiny.

Connecting the Dots: A Universal Truth

When we look at Yin and Yang, the principle of "you reap what you sow," Newton's third law, and the concept of Karma, it becomes clear that these diverse ideas all point to a universal truth: our actions have consequences. Whether through the lens of philosophy, religion, or science, the message is the same—what we do matters, and it will come back to us in some way.

This realization reminds us that we are in control of our actions, and therefore, we have a say in the outcomes of our lives. It also teaches us the importance of living in balance, making wise decisions, and treating others with kindness and respect.

Whether you call it Karma, the law of action and reaction, or simply the balance of life, this universal truth reminds us to live with intention, mindfulness, and integrity.

Yin-Yang, Action-Reaction, You reap what you sow, and karma, all point to a universal law: the unity of opposites. Two opposing forces (+/-) are bound together and are unified as one. The Tao symbol itself is a representation of that unity, as well as the iron tool that opened the mouth of the gods (magnet) which is a physical proof of that unity.

The Light and Dark Sides of the Force in Star Wars

There is a direct reference of the unity concept in the movies. Star Wars explains "the dark side of the force." After all, there is a dark and light side of the force. There can't be good without evil. and they are one.

In the Star Wars movies, the concept of the Force is central to the story. The Force is an energy field that connects everything in the universe. It has two sides: the Light Side, which represents good, and the Dark Side, which represents evil. These two sides are often seen as opposing forces, much like good and evil in the real world.

However, the deeper message in "Star Wars" is that these two sides are actually part of the same whole. You can't have one without the other. Just like day and night, or hot and cold, the Light Side and Dark Side of the Force exist together, creating balance in the universe.

For example, in the movies, characters like Anakin Skywalker struggle with this balance. He starts as a Jedi, following the Light Side, but is tempted by the power of the Dark Side. His journey shows that even a good person can be drawn to evil, and that both sides are within us all.

This idea is similar to concepts found in some Eastern philosophies, where opposing forces, like yin and yang, are seen as interconnected and necessary for harmony. In Star Wars, the struggle between the Light and Dark Sides of the Force reflects this balance, and it reminds us that good and evil are two parts of the same reality; not separate things.

If you have watched the movie, you would know that the story isn't just about good guys fighting bad guys. It's about understanding that both good and evil are part of the same universe, and that finding balance between them is key to understanding ourselves and the world around us.

I have a great admiration for the eastern religions. They share so much in common, but my favorite part is how they approach the opposing forces in nature. The positive and negative are intertwined and related to one another. You can't have one without the other. This is unity. This is in contrast to the western religions, which present the opposing forces as separate (god, devil), and are unrelated adversaries. One must choose between one and the other. This attitude fails to accept that each of these forces, positive and negative are part of us. The "devil" is not some outside entity but is a force that lives within us along with the good. It is our choice how we respond to these forces.

This is the key to the problem. Opposing forces are at work in the universe and yet they are somehow related. This duality is also present in science, especially physics.

Physics primary goal is to explain the inner workings of the universe using the scientific method, and find the source of all things.

The unity of opposite concept can be found not only in nature but also in modern physics. Examples are electricity and magnetism. They both involve the binary of positive and negative, which are bound together. At the subatomic level particles are created and destroyed, but the energy remains constant. Another example is in wave and particle physics. At the atomic level, matter has duality since it appears as particles and as waves.

To the physicist and eastern mystic, reality transcends the duality of opposites. In Physics, quantum mechanics, the uncertainty principle describes the mathematical inequalities describing a fundamental limit to how accurate values for the physical quantities of particles such as position and momentum can be predicted. In the Upanishads where it said, "It moves, it moves not. It is far, it is near. It is within all this and it is outside all this." This is a mystical way of saying the same thing. Another example is quantum entanglement. This is a fuzzy concept. It describes what happens when a group of particles interact or share spatial proximity in such a way that the quantum state of each particle of the group cannot be described independently of the state of the others even when the particles are separated by a long distance. This suggests an instantaneous relationship that exists between the particles, faster than light. There appears to be an underlying force that acts on them at the same time. Einstein called this spooky at a distance. There is an excellent book by Fritjof Capra titled "The Tao of Physics", which was published in January, 1976. which gives a detailed description of how the eastern concept of Tao is expressed in physics. Physics seeks to understand the universe and it's laws. Physics is the endeavor of seeing the essential nature of all things.

This connection between physics and Eastern mysticism suggests that the more we learn about the universe through science, the closer we come to the truths that ancient spiritual traditions have been pointing to for millennia. It reinforces the idea that the fundamental nature of reality is one of unity, where opposites are not in conflict but are complementary parts of a greater whole.

In essence, both science and spirituality teach us that the universe operates on a principle of balance and interconnectedness. Our actions, whether physical, moral, or spiritual, have far-reaching consequences, not just in our immediate surroundings but in the very fabric of reality itself. Understanding this can lead us to live more harmoniously with the world around us, embracing the unity of all things, and recognizing the profound impact of our choices.

THE TIE THAT BINDS

After I did my research on Eastern and Western religions, I noticed the conflict between the two. The main conflict is that Western religions put a lot of emphasis on God and the Devil as enemies, while Eastern religions do not. The Eastern religions recognize that two opposite forces are tied together—one side cannot exist without the other. When I became aware of the ancient Egyptians' religious teachings, I noticed they used similar concepts as the Eastern religions to describe the same thing. I also found the Egyptian religion to be the root of many Western religious teachings and concepts. I believe the Egyptians are the binding tie between Western and Eastern religions.

My first real clue about the origins of Jewish and Christian religions was reading about Moses. I found it interesting that Moses grew up in the royal Egyptian court. Given that, he would have acquired detailed knowledge and concepts of the Egyptian gods. I believe when he left Egypt, he took with him the best of that Egyptian knowledge and incorporated it into the Jewish faith. Jesus was also hiding in Egypt during his early years as a child. He, too, would have been exposed to the Egyptian religion.

In the Egyptian Book of the Dead and related texts, I found stories similar to those in the Bible. For example, I found the story of a god-like person named Osiris who rose from the dead after his brutal murder. Instead of the Virgin Mary, there was Isis.

The Egyptians believed that all life on earth owed its existence to a central power, represented physically as the sun. Life was represented as the Ankh, and the universe (earth) was represented as the Tet. They all combined to express the idea that all life on earth is part of the source of life. These symbols are combined above.

A lot of emphasis was placed on the passing of the spirit of a person to the afterworld after death. The Egyptians had a complex burial ritual, which was performed after death using Osiris as the example.

The heart of the dead was balanced against the feather of the law by the god Anubis, the god of balance. This was done before Osiris, and the opening of the mouth was performed with the iron tool that opened the mouth of the gods.

The Egyptians used gods to describe different aspects of nature. Most served a specific function. After reading about them, I could see the relationship between them, and I noticed they all formed a system. A basic diagram is given below.

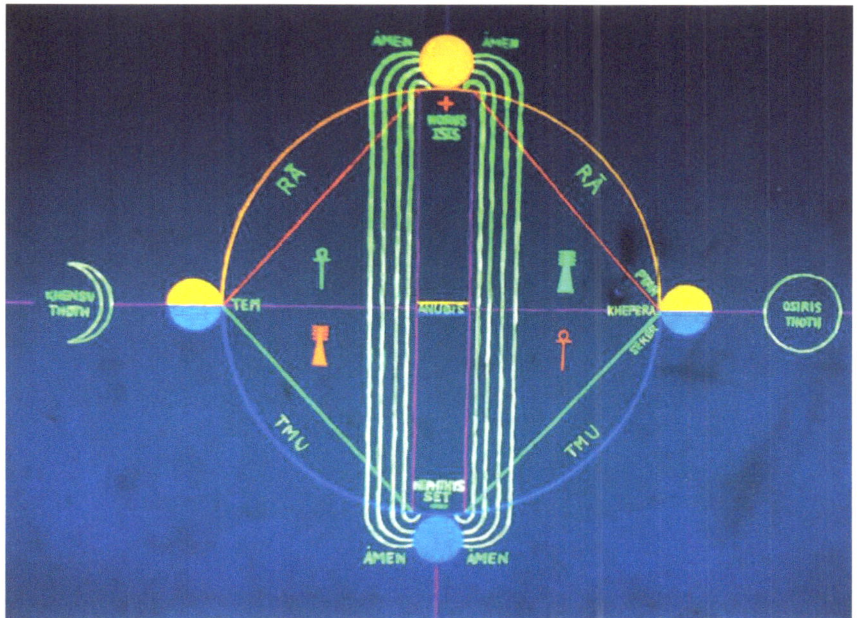

In the diagram above, note that the most important feature is the depiction of a magnet with its opposite poles defined by specific Egyptian gods. This will be shown to be the iron tool that opened the mouth of the gods. I will describe this in more detail along with its mention in the Bible.

Note in the diagram the names on top represent the positive aspects, and on the bottom, the negative aspects. In the middle is the god of balance, Anubis. The Avatar Osiris is the full moon, and the messenger god Khensu is the new moon. From the magnet, we can see the polarity of opposites through Horus-Set, and the unifying force between them, the Amen.

The dual god Horus-Set is depicted with two heads: Horus on the right, and Set on the left. In Egyptian mythology, they were known as the "combatant gods," each side fighting with the other in a pitched battle back and forth, with Horus dominating and then Set, but neither able to destroy the other. This is a similar concept as expressed in the Tao symbol.

The dual god Horus-Set, along with Anubis, god of balance, were part of the sacred burial ceremony. It depicted the weighing of the heart, which represented the conscience balanced against the feather of the law. Part of the ceremony was the opening of the mouth with the iron tool that opened the mouth of the gods.

In the battle of the combatant gods, the god Thoth, who was lord of divine words, served as the arbitrator. Thoth, the lord of Maat, master of law and truth, was tasked with preventing either god from gaining a decisive victory and destroying the other. His duty was to keep these hostile forces in exact equilibrium—the forces being light and darkness, day and night, or good and evil.

During the opening of the mouth, the Osiris of a man enters into heaven as a living soul. He is regarded as one of those who "have eaten the eye of Horus" and walks among the living ones. He becomes "God, son of God," and all the gods of heaven become his brethren. His bones are the gods and goddesses of heaven. His right side belongs to Horus, his left side to Set, and his face to Anubis.

"Thy mouth was closed, but I have set in order for thee thy mouth and teeth. I open for thee thy mouth; I have opened for thee thy two eyes. I have opened for thee thy mouth with the instrument of Anubis. I have opened thy mouth with the instrument of Anubis, with the iron tool with which the mouths of the gods were opened. Horus (+) opens the mouth, Horus opens the mouth. Horus opens the mouth of the dead, as he whilom opened the mouth of Osiris, with the iron which came forth from Set (-) with the iron tool with which he opened the mouths of the gods."

More references to duality occur in the Egyptian Book of the Dead by E.A. Wallis Budge:

"Thou hast gotten possession of the eyes of Horus, the White and the Black. Thou hast taken them unto thyself, and they illume thy face." – page cxl

"O grant that the two lands which rejoiced to do homage with Horus may do homage unto Set." – Page cxli

"Horus purifieth and Set strengtheneth, and Set purifieth and Horus strengtheneth." – Page 290

The continuous reference to Horus-Set and the concept they represent was a key component of the duality of nature expressed in the Egyptian religion.

These texts show the relationship of duality and balance and tie them to an iron tool. The only iron tool with the properties described is a magnet. It is a physical representation of the unity of opposites.

There are some subtle ties to the iron tool in the Bible and the Book of Mormon.

From the Douay-Rheims version of the Bible, The Apocalypse Chapter 19 Verse 15: "And out of his mouth proceedeth a sharp two-edged sword; that with it he may strike the nations. And he shall rule them with a rod of iron; and he treadeth the winepress of the fierceness of wrath of God the Almighty."

From the Book of Mormon, Nephi Chapter 8 Verses 19, 23, and 24: "And I beheld a rod of iron, and it extended along the bank of the river, and it led to the tree by which I stood... And it came to pass there arose a mist of darkness; and yea, even as the extending great mist of darkness, insomuch that they who had commenced in the path did lose their way and wandered off and were lost. And it came to pass that I beheld others pressing forward, and they came forth and caught hold of the end of the rod of iron; and they did press forward through the mist of darkness, clinging to the rod of iron, even until they came forth and partook of the fruit of the tree."

Also in Chapter 15 Verses 23 and 24: "And they said unto me: What meaneth the rod of iron which our father saw, that led to the tree? And I said unto them that it was the word of God; and whoso would harken unto the word of God and would hold fast unto it, they would never perish."

At first glance, it appeared that the Egyptians practiced polytheism (many gods) instead of monotheism (one god). In reality, theirs was a symbolic system that had a single god, the "king of the gods," and the name of this god was Amen-Ra. All the other gods represented avatars, concepts, or different aspects of nature.

In the previous diagram, the magnetic field between the two opposing forces, Horus-Set, represents the underlying unifying force between them, the Amen.

Amen means "the hidden one," and the name became the personification of the creating and sustaining force of the universe, which in material form was typified by the sun (Ra). Above is a picture of Amen-Ra and its many attributes.

There is a direct reference to Amen in the Douay-Rheims version of the Bible. The Apocalypse Chapter 3 Verse 14: "And to the angel of the church of Laodicea write: These things saith the Amen, the faithful and true witness, who is the beginning of the creation of God." In the footnote of this verse, it says, "The Amen, that is, the true one, the Truth itself; the Word and Son of God. Ibid. The beginning, that is the principle, the source and efficient cause of the whole creation."

By definition, the meaning of Amen is the same in the Douay-Rheims version of the Bible as it is in Egyptian texts.

Amen appears to be a name for God, not just an affirmation. Using the magnet, or "rod of iron," the basic law of the universe is expressed. Use the unity of opposites concept to help achieve Nirvana and liberation. Maintain the balance in your life and in nature.

www.ingramcontent.com/pod-product-compliance
Lightning Source LLC
Chambersburg PA
CBHW041739300726
48978CB00006B/163